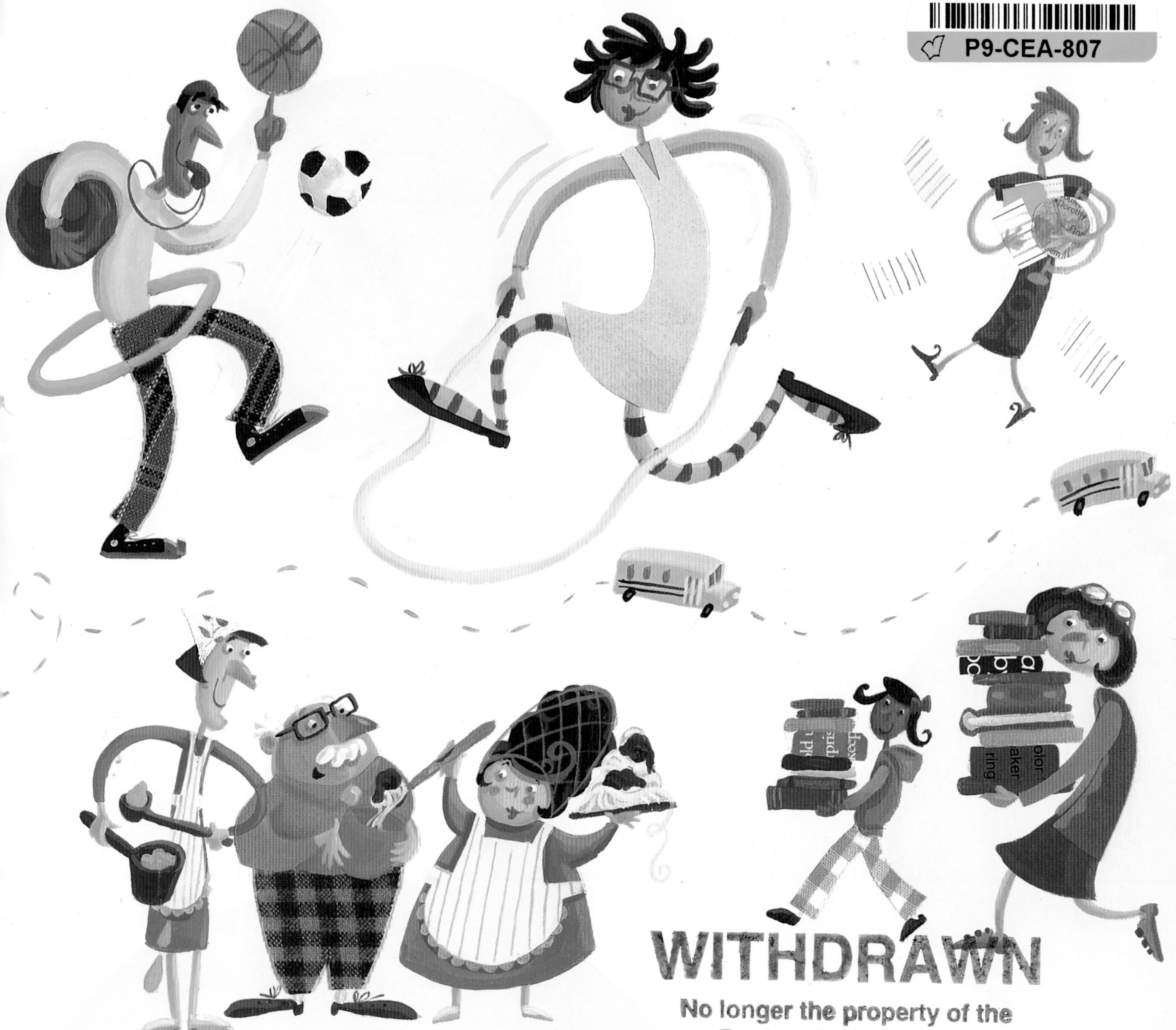

For the boys—James, Daniel, Michael, and, of course, Chris —M.A.M.

Text copyright © 2006 by Mary-Alice Moore • Illustrations copyright © 2006 by Laura Huliska-Beith • Musical arrangement copyright © 2006 by Marlene Hajdu • Manufactured in China. • All rights reserved. www.harperchildrens.com • Library of Congress Cataloging-in-Publication Data • Moore, Mary-Alice. • The wheels on the school bus / written by Mary-Alice Moore ; illustrated by Laura Huliska-Beith.— 1st ed. • p. cm. • Summary: Text adapted from the traditional song describes how students and staff ride the bus to school. • ISBN-10: 0-06-059427-6 (trade) — ISBN-13: 978-0-06-059427-5 (trade) — ISBN-10: 0-06-059428-4 (lib. bdg.) ISBN-13: 978-0-06-059428-2 (lib. bdg.) • 1. Children's songs, English—United States—Texts. [1. School buses—Songs and music. 2. Songs.] I. Huliska-Beith, Laura, ill. II. Title. • PZ8.3.M7838Wh 2006 • [782.42]—dc22 •2004013207 • CIP • AC • Typography by Stephanie Bart-Horvath • ❖
1 2 3 4 5 6 7 8 9 10 • ❖
First Edition

For Anna, Isaac, Connor, Gabriel, and Joseph. Happy School Days! —L.H.B

HarperCollinsPublishers

The Wheels on the Schoolbus

Written by Mary-Alice Moore

Illustrated by Laura Huliska-Beith

The wheels on the bus go round and round,
Round and round, round and round.
The wheels on the bus go round and round
All the way to school.

The kids on the bus say,

"Off to school! Here we go! Off to school!"

The kids on the bus say,

"Here we go!"

All the way to school.

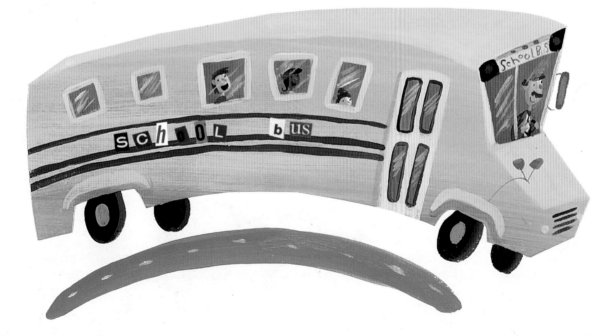

The teachers on the bus say,
"Think, think, think!
Learn, learn, learn!
Think, think, think!"
The teachers on the bus say,
"Learn, learn, learn!"
All the way to school.

MIRROR

The librarian on the bus says,
"Read, read, read! Books, books, books!
Read, read, read!"
The librarian on the bus says,
"Read more books!"
All the way to school.

TURBO TURTLE
SPEEDOMETER

SCHOOL HOME
COMPASS

OPEN CLOSED
DOORS

ON OFF
FLOTATION DEVICE

EJECT

The coach on the bus says,
"Catch, catch, catch! Throw, throw, throw!
Catch, catch, catch!"
The coach on the bus says,
"Throw, throw, throw!"
All the way to school.

The nurse on the bus says,
"Open wide! **A**aah, aaah, aaah!
Open wide!"
The nurse on the bus says,
"**A**aah, aaah, aaah!"
All the way to school.

The lunch ladies on the bus say,
"Eat! Eat! Eat! Yum, yum, yum!
Eat! Eat! Eat!"
The lunch ladies on the bus say,
"Let's eat lunch!"
All the way to school.

The music teacher on the bus says,
"Sing, sing, sing! Play, play, play!
Sing, sing, sing!"
The music teacher on the bus sings,
"Do re mi . . ."
All the way to school.

The art teacher on the bus says,
"Paint, paint, paint! Draw, draw, draw!
Paint, paint, paint!"
The art teacher on the bus says,
"Draw, draw, draw!"
All the way to school.

The custodian on the bus says,
"Mop, mop, mop! Sweep, sweep, sweep!
Mop, mop, mop!"
The custodian on the bus says,
"Clean this mess!"
All the way to school.

The driver on the bus says,
"Everybody off! Everybody off! Everybody off!"
The driver on the bus says,
"Here we are!
Welcome to my school!"

The Wheels on the Bus

Lyrics by Mary-Alice Moore

Arranged by Marlene Hajdu